Favorite Fairy Tales
Snow White
And The Seven Dwarfs

Retold by Rochelle Larkin   Illustrated by Nan Brooks

CREATIVE CHILD PRESS
is a registered trademark of Playmore Inc.,
Publishers and Waldman Publishing Corp., New York, N.Y.

Once upon a time in a far away kingdom lived a beautiful princess named Snow White, her father, the king, and her cruel stepmother, the new queen. Everyone loved the good little princess, everyone except her stepmother.

Each day the queen would look in her magic mirror and ask, "Mirror, mirror, on the wall, who's the fairest one of all?" The mirror would answer, "You are, my queen."

But one day the mirror answered, "Snow White is the fairest in the land." It was true. Princess Snow White had grown to be the loveliest girl in the kingdom.

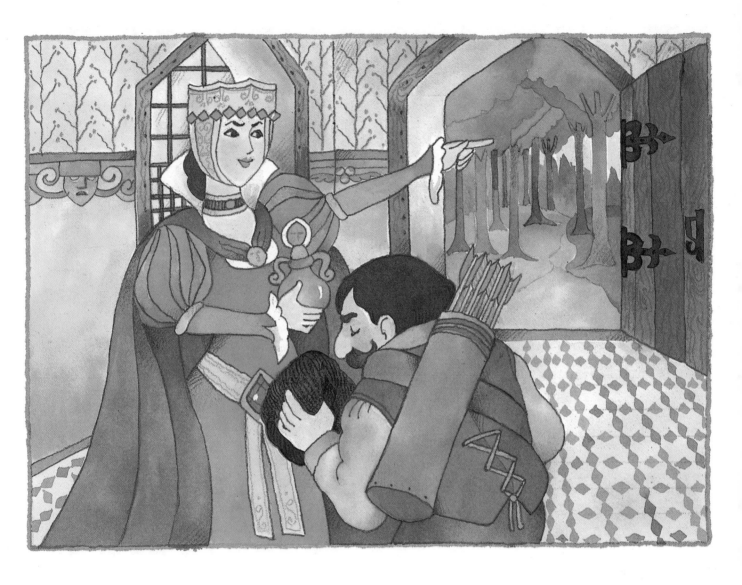

The queen wanted to get rid of Snow White. She made a woodsman lead the princess into the deepest part of the forest and leave her there.

Snow White tried to be brave. She looked for a way out of the forest. Instead she found a tiny cottage almost hidden in some tall pine trees. She stepped inside.

Everything in the cottage was neat and shiny-clean, but as tiny as anything Snow White had ever seen. And even more amazing, there was seven of everything! Snow White was tired from her long walk in the forest. She fell asleep across the seven little beds.

While she slept, the sound of marching boots and a hearty song stirred the forest outside. The owners of the cottage were coming home. They were the seven dwarfs, coming home from work, led by their chief, One-a-Dwarf.

"Someone is sleeping on our beds!" said Two-a-Dwarf as they marched inside. Snow White woke up with a start.

"Who are you? Where do you come from? What are you doing in our house?" all the dwarfs began asking at once.

When Snow White told them what the evil queen had done, they felt sorry for her.

"You can stay here with us," Three-a-Dwarf said after the dwarfs had talked among themselves.

Snow White agreed to stay and take care of the house while the dwarfs were at work. Every day she cheerfully tended the cottage and garden. One day, as she worked inside, a strange woman came by. She carried a basket of apples.

"Good morning, my pretty," the woman called through the open window. "Wouldn't you like one of my shiny red apples?"

The dwarfs had told Snow White never to let anyone into the cottage. Snow White didn't know that the woman was the queen in disguise. She was standing outside, and the apples looked so good.

The woman went away, and Snow White went back to her chores. But soon she grew very, very tired. She lay down to rest.

When the dwarfs came home that night, they found Snow White stretched out on the bed they had made for her. She was completely still, barely breathing. On the floor was the core of the apple she had eaten.

One-a-Dwarf sniffed the apple core. He passed it to each of the dwarfs in turn.

"Poison!" said Three-a-Dwarf. "Poison!" said Six-a-Dwarf. Each of the dwarfs echoed the sad news. Someone had poisoned their darling Snow White.

"See how pale she is, yet she breathes," said
Four-a-Dwarf. "She's only sleeping."

"But a great, deep sleep," said the wise Three-a-Dwarf.

"Oh, dear me," said Five-a-Dwarf.

"Whatever shall we do?" asked little Seven-a-Dwarf.

The dwarfs built a special bed for Snow White, with a great glass cover, so they could watch over her. They set it in the flower garden she had loved so much.

Not many people came to that part of the forest, but those who did told the tale of the beautiful young girl who lay long asleep there.

A brave young prince, traveling from a far-off land, heard the story and decided to see for himself. He rode through the forest until he came to the dwarfs' cottage.

When he saw Snow White, she looked so beautiful
that he knelt down and kissed her.

All at once, Snow White began to stir.
She opened her eyes and beheld the young prince.

As she sat up, the dwarfs shouted and cheered. Snow White had been saved by love's first kiss!

The kiss broke the evil queen's spell and all of her other powers as well.

And Snow White and her prince lived happily ever after.